Christy

Christmastime
at Cutter Gap

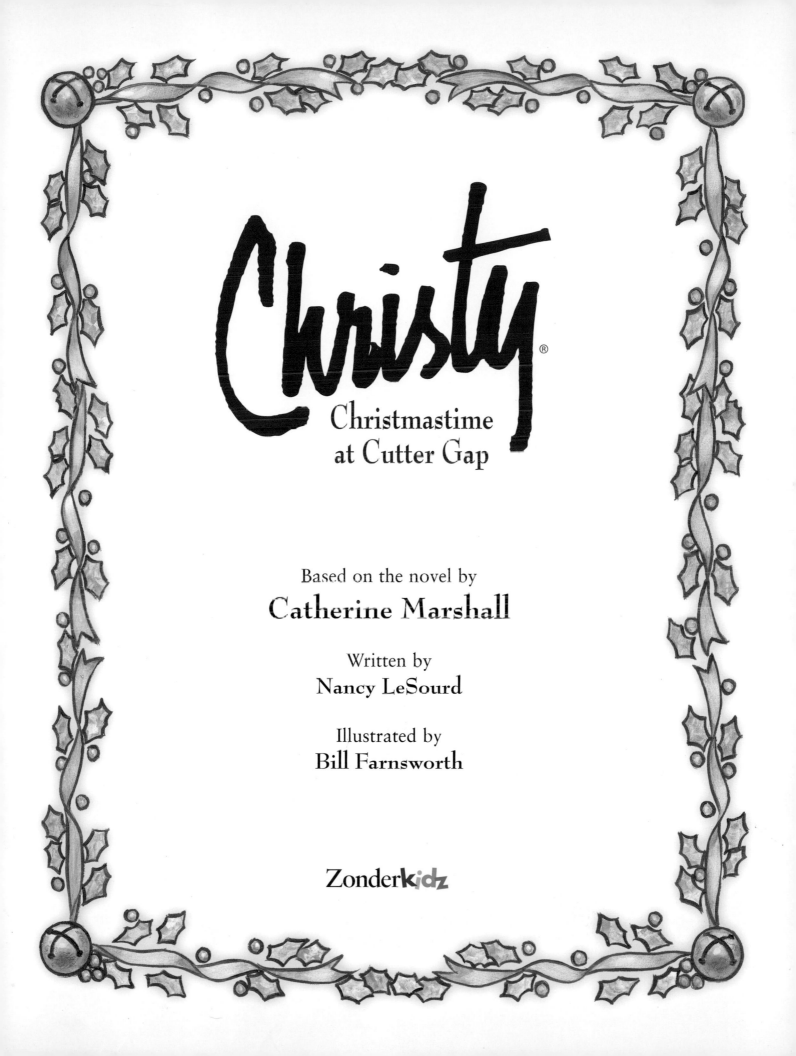

Christy®

Christmastime
at Cutter Gap

Based on the novel by
Catherine Marshall

Written by
Nancy LeSourd

Illustrated by
Bill Farnsworth

Zonderkidz

Zonder**kidz**.

The children's group of Zondervan

www.zonderkidz.com

Christy: Christmastime at Cutter Gap
ISBN: 0-310-70571-1
Copyright © 2003 by Nancy LeSourd
Illustrations copyright © 2003 by Marshall-LeSourd L.L.C.

Requests for information should be addressed to:
Zonderkidz, Grand Rapids, Michigan 49530

Produced in association with the brand development agency of Evergreen
Ideas, Inc. on behalf of Marshall-LeSourd L. L. C.

Editor: Gwen Ellis
Interior Design and Art Direction: Laura M. Maitner

Printed in China
03 04 05 06/HK/4 3 2 1

For the grandchildren and
great-grandchildren of
Catherine Marshall LeSourd
Nancy LeSourd

To my daughter Allison,
who posed as the Christy model.
B.F.

Christy Huddleston closed her book and said, "It's time for our Christmas holiday." The children squealed with delight. "Wait a minute!" urged Miss Christy. "Before we leave, I want to hear what your families have planned for Christmas."

Zacharias and his brother, Wraight, jumped up and strutted around the schoolroom, gobbling and flapping their arms. "We're goin' turkey hunting with Pa to try to bag a big ol' bird for our Christmas dinner."

The children laughed and clapped—all except one, Ruby Mae. Folks in the Cove claimed that Ruby Mae chattered so much she could talk water uphill. But today she wasn't saying a word.

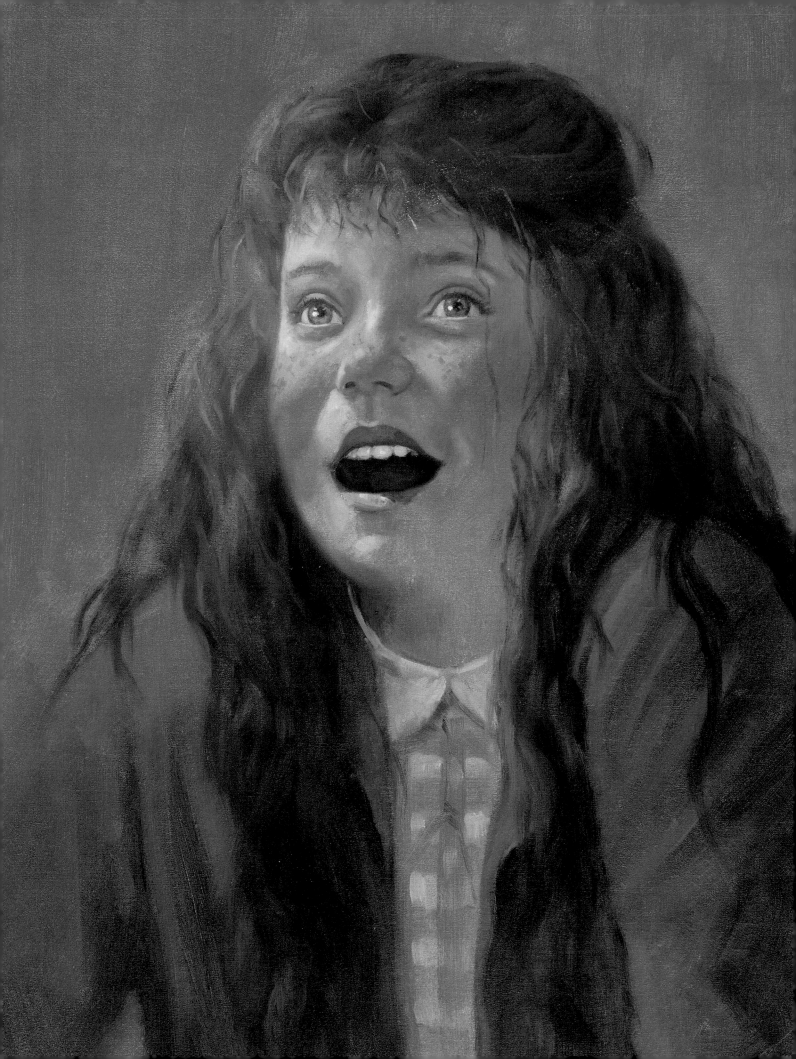

Miss Christy called on John, the oldest of the Spencer children. "We make honeycomb pies from a secret recipe our grandmama gave us."

"And I get to help," added Clara Spencer. "I'm ten now and a growed-up woman. Mama says it's time for me to learn the secret pie recipe."

"I'm spending Christmas with Pa." The words exploded out of Ruby Mae's mouth.

Everyone stopped talking and just looked at her. They all knew Ruby Mae's pa had not lived in the Cove since her ma died. Ruby Mae lived at the Mission House now.

Christy asked quietly, "You're not spending Christmas at the Mission House?"

Ruby Mae bit her lip, took a deep breath, shook her head, and said, "No, Miss Christy. I'll be spending Christmas with Pa in our old cabin."

The room was suddenly very quiet. Finally Miss Christy said, "Have a wonderful Christmas, Class! You are dismissed."

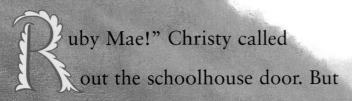R uby Mae!" Christy called out the schoolhouse door. But Ruby Mae had already started up the trail to the mountain. She did not hear her teacher's voice.

"Teacher, I'm worried about Ruby Mae," said Clara Spencer, who was standing nearby. "I don't think her pa's up there."

"Now, don't you worry, Clara," Miss Christy said, giving her a hug. "I'm going to check on Ruby Mae this afternoon as soon as I can. You had best get on home and get started on those honeycomb pies."

After an hour of hard walking up the mountain, Ruby Mae came to her family's old cabin. It was in worse condition than she had remembered. The door was hanging by one hinge. Piles of leaves and broken branches were scattered on the floor. An old table, one chair, and a few blankets were piled in a corner.

She sighed, then went to work. When she finished, she took two small rolls from her pocket and placed them in a cracked bowl in the center of the table. Standing back, she looked at the clean cabin. *Hmmm. Something's missing,* she thought.

"Oh, I know," she said, grabbing a rusty old ax as she ran out of the cabin and down the trail. She spotted a scrawny pine tree that was not much taller than she was and chopped it down. Ruby Mae dragged the evergreen into the cabin and propped it against a wall. "Now what can I use for decorations?" she asked herself. Ruby Mae found some red rags, tore them into strips, and tied the strips onto the limbs of the tree. "There," she said, "the perfect Christmas tree."

Soon snow began to fall and the wind began to howl. Ruby Mae built a small fire in the fireplace and huddled close for warmth. But it didn't help much. The brown oilcloth at the window slapped and flapped in the icy wind. She pulled her sweater around her tightly and stamped her feet to shake off the chill.

Maybe if I sing a Christmas carol I won't feel so cold and alone, she thought. Her voice cracked, and she started to cry.

Then she prayed. "Oh, Lord, I've really made a mess of things. I told everyone I was spending Christmas with Pa. But he don't care none about me. I ain't even seen him in a year. If I had just kept my mouth shut, I'd be at the Mission House eating Miss Ida's Christmas cake and listening to Miss Christy and Reverend Grantland singing songs at the piano." Ruby Mae sat very still. The only sound in the cabin besides the wind was her own breathing.

The fire had burned down to just a few small embers. Night was coming soon. Ruby Mae decided she'd better get some more firewood. Wrapping one of the blankets tightly around her shoulders, Ruby Mae set off in search of wood.

In almost no time, she found three good-sized logs and some kindling. She went slowly back up the trail to the cabin, struggling under her load. Suddenly she slipped on the icy path. The logs flew out of her arms, and Ruby Mae banged her head hard on the cabin steps. She lay motionless in the snow as the sun began to set.

Coming up through the forest, Christy urged her horse, Buttons, onward. It was getting dark, and the snow was coming down faster now. She had to find Ruby Mae quickly.

She urged the horse around one more corner, and there in the clearing was the Morrisons' cabin. She rode up close to it, and then she saw something—or someone—lying in the snow, right by the cabin door. "Ruby Mae!" Christy yelled, jumping down from the saddle. She ran to the girl and brushed the snow from her face. Ruby Mae was breathing, but she was very, very still.

I have to get her someplace warm, Christy thought as she struggled to lift Ruby Mae onto Buttons' back. When she was secure, Christy climbed on behind her and wrapped her arms around Ruby Mae's waist. "It's okay, Ruby Mae, I've got you now. Let's go, Buttons."

Christy headed for the nearest cabin—the Spencer's place. It took Buttons only a few minutes to plow through the snow and pass through the Spencer's front gate. The door flew open just as they reached the porch, and Mrs. Spencer exclaimed, "Miss Christy! Is that Ruby Mae? What happened?"

"I don't know, Fairlight. She has a big bump on her head."

Mr. Spencer ran out of the cabin right behind his wife. He quickly but gently lifted Ruby Mae down, carried her inside, and carefully placed her onto the bed. Fairlight Spencer tenderly covered her with warm blankets.

All the Spencer children gathered around as Christy began wiping Ruby
Mae's forehead with a cool cloth. Lulu asked, "When she gonna
wake up, Teacher?"

Christy replied, "I don't know. But while she's sleeping, why don't you
think of something we can do to make her Christmas very, very special."

Lulu brightened. "I can make her a pretty card!"

John offered, "I'll write a story."

Clara said, "I know, Teacher. I'll give her my very best honeycomb pie."

"Those are great ideas, children," replied Christy. "Now you get busy and say a little prayer for Ruby Mae while you work."

It was very quiet in the cabin while the children worked on their surprises. Then Bang! Bang! Bang! Everyone jumped as the door rattled with the pounding. Mr. Spencer opened the door to find a man covered in snow from head to toe.

"Why, Mr. Morrison!" exclaimed Mr. Spencer. "Come in an warm yerself. Yer gonna catch yer death of cold out there." Mr. Morrison shook the snow from his boots and coat before stepping into the warm cabin.

"Mighty obliged," he replied. "I was on my way to the Mission House to see my daughter, Ruby Mae, and thought I might say howdy—it being Christmas Eve and all."

Thank God you're here," said Christy as she took Mr. Morrison by the arm. "You came just in time. Ruby Mae, is here. She fell up at your cabin and banged her head. She's been unconscious, but I think she's coming around now."

Christy was right. Ruby Mae was rubbing her eyes and trying to sit up in bed. "Take it easy, Ruby Mae. You've had a nasty bump on your head." said Christy.

Finally Ruby Mae got her eyes partway open. "Pa?" Ruby Mae asked very softly.

Christy hurried over to him and whispered, "Mr. Morrison, come and sit by Ruby Mae. She needs you."

Mr. Morrison hesitated. Then his mouth quivered, and he wiped at a tear rolling down his cheek. "What Ruby Mae needs," he said, "is her mother. Ain't right she got no ma."

Christy said gently, "I know, but she has you. Please, Mr. Morrison. Please come be with your daughter."

hristy led Mr. Morrison to the chair near the head of Ruby Mae's bed. Then Mr. Spencer asked, "Miss Christy, would you read us the Christmas story from the Good Book?"

"Oh yes, please, Miss Christy. Read to us about the angels telling the shepherds that Jesus was born," begged Lulu.

"And about all the commotion in heaven 'cause they were so happy." added Clara.

Christy laughed and said, "Lulu, you're as excited as the angels were that first Christmas night!" Then she opened her Bible and read: "The angel said to them, 'Do not be afraid. I bring you good news of great joy. It is for all the people. Today in the town of David a Savior has been born to you. He is Christ the Lord.'"

When Christy finished reading the Christmas story, she asked, "Does anyone know why God sent Jesus to be born in the first place?"

"To show us how to live a good life?" answered Clara.

"To teach us how to love each other?" answered John.

"Well, those are all very good thoughts, but God tells us in the Bible that God can't be where there is sin. Our sin has separated us from him. But God loves us so much that he wants us to be with him forever. So he gave us Jesus as a gift to remove our sin. That way we can be together again."

Christy was watching Mr. Morrison's face as she went on. "When we give each other gifts at Christmastime, we are celebrating the greatest gift of all—Jesus! We can reject God's free gift—he won't force us to take it—but he surely hopes we will take it, because he is a loving heavenly Father who wants us to be with him forever."

Christy was quiet for a moment, then she said, "Now speaking of gifts, who has a present for Ruby Mae?"

One by one, each of the Spencer children gave Ruby Mae the gifts they had made for her. She was so excited with all the attention and surprises that she could hardly sit still. Her father watched as she opened and held up each present for all to see.

Then after the last gift had been opened, Mr. Morrison stood up. Ruby Mae suddenly got very quiet. She whispered, "Please ... please, don't go." A tear slid down her cheek, and she squeezed her eyes tightly to stop any more tears from slipping out. She needed to be very brave if her father was leaving again.

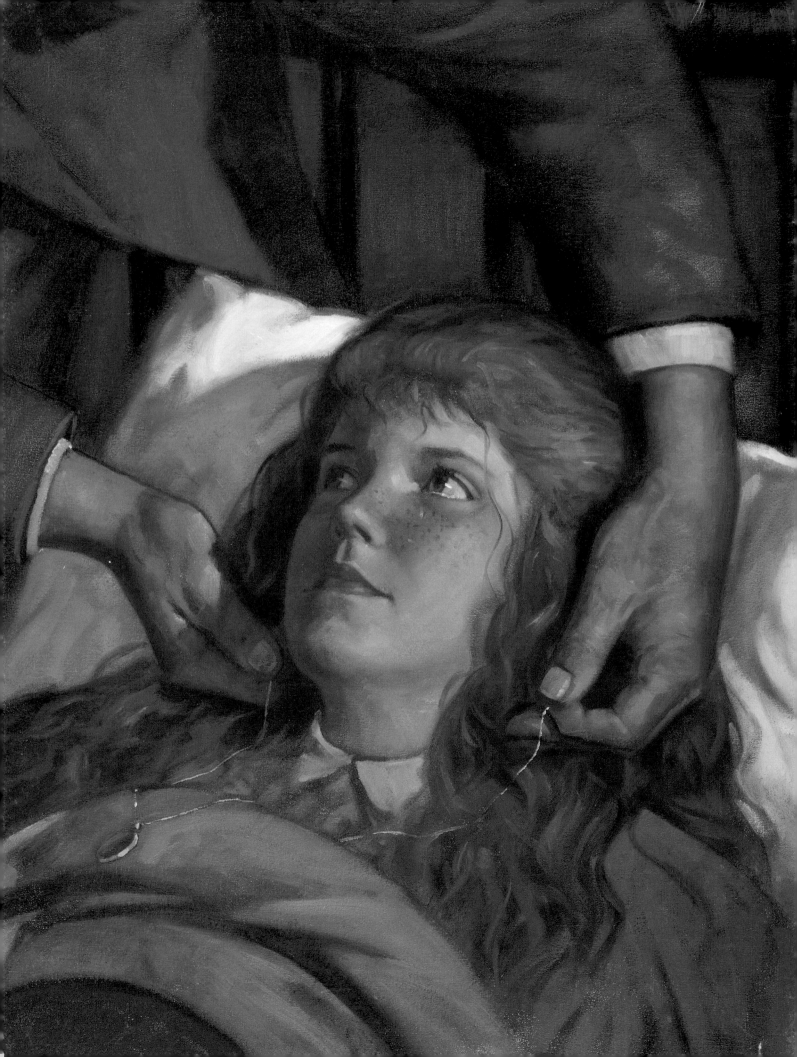

Then while her eyes were still shut, Ruby Mae felt her father's rough fingers gently brush her hair away from her neck. Something cold touched her skin as her father fumbled with something at the back of her neck. Slowly she lifted her hand and touched a locket on a chain. She turned slowly and looked at her father, her face full of questions. "Your Christmas present, Ruby Mae," he explained. "It was your mama's, and now I want you to have it."

"But … but … you said you never wanted to see it again."

"I've changed my mind. I want to see it now, on you, at Christmas." Mr. Morrison brushed the back of his hand over his eyes to keep a tear from tumbling out. "Something Miss Christy said about God's love and all … well, it just settled deep down inside me. I've made plenty of mistakes, Ruby Mae, but the worst one was thinking that if I just forgot about you, I could forget the pain of losing your ma. I'm sorry I hurt you, and I'm wondering if … will you forgive me?"

Ruby Mae threw her arms around her father and exclaimed, "Forgive you, Pa? Why, I already have! And this necklace is the perfect Christmas present ... for a perfect Christmas. It's perfect because you are here and all ... not 'cause I got a present ... but I love this present ... being Mama's and all. And I love honeycomb pie." Ruby Mae continued to chatter incessantly about the wonderful smells in the Spencer house, the decorated tree, the snow, the Christmas carols, and anything else that popped into her mind.

"Well, Mr. Morrison," Christy laughed, "I think we have our old Ruby Mae back! Merry Christmas!"

"Merry Christmas, Miss Christy. Merry Christmas indeed!" replied Mr. Morrison, and a small smile appeared at the corners of his mouth as he scooped up Ruby Mae in his strong arms and gave her a kiss on her cheek. Ruby Mae was so stunned that even she stopped talking—well, for a moment anyway.